Under the Big Oak Tree

A Children's Book About Life Lessons Using Imagination and Creativity

JOHN W. POWELL

TABLE OF CONTENTS

DEDICATION AND ACKNOWLEDGEMENTS

I would like to dedicate this book to Vickie, my wife; Leota Powell, my mom; and Carrie Smith, my aunt.

The people mentioned above are so special because they are the most influential people in my life. My wife, Vickie, has stuck by my side through thick and thin. She has been very supportive to me in the writing of this book. My mother, Leota, who is no longer with us, was loving and caring.

My Aunt Carrie, who raised me, was also a loving and caring mother.

The special message I want to send to the people I'm dedicating this book to is: Thank you for loving and believing in me throughout the years. There is absolutely no doubt in my mind and heart of your love for me.

I would like to thank my wife Vickie for her dedication to and support of me as I prepared this manuscript. Many thanks to the staff of Motivational MD who greatly assisted and encouraged me as I wrote this book. Many thanks to Kent Dorsey for providing the pictures for my book.

My special message to the people above is: You have helped to inspire me in the writing of this book.

Thank you very much.

1

INTRODUCTION

Hi, my name is John Powell, and I am an author and youth inspirational speaker. This book is focused on reaching elementary students, and my goal is to share with them some of my life experiences as a child.

In this book, children will learn how to use their imagination in a fun and creative way. They will also learn how to stretch their imagination, originality, and creativity, and to think outside of the box as well as reach their highest potential. I want children to be able to glean from the life lessons presented in these short stories. It's education for children away from social media, electronics, etc.

This book also consists of some daring, exciting and challenging experiences, along with entertainment for their young minds. At the end of each chapter, there are thoughtful questions and reflections to stimulate their thinking and promote discussion.

2

UNDER THE BIG OAK TREE

I didn't have a lot of toys when I was a little boy, so I came up with the idea of using acorn tops to play cowboys and Indians under the big oak tree. I was all alone and had plenty of room to roam.

I pretended the acorn tops were men, and I used mayonnaise jar tops as stagecoaches and covered wagons. There were many battles between the cowboys and Indians, and the acorn tops were broken up into many pieces, indicating that they went to their deaths in battle.

I can remember being attacked by a mean old rooster while playing under the big oak tree. He jumped on me and his sharp claws dug into my head, causing me to bleed. I was crying and screaming. I was so afraid. My mom quickly came to my rescue and chased away the rooster. She took me into the house, cleaned up the cut and put a Band-Aid on it.

She promised me that she was going to get rid of that mean old rooster. Guess what she did about a week later? She had a fence built around the chicken house so that the rooster and hens would no longer run free in our yard or under the big oak tree. I was happy and free to play again without being afraid of being attacked by that mean old rooster. My favorite of all the memories I experienced while playing under the big oak tree was enjoying total peace and happiness. I learned that scary things don't last forever. When you're poor, lonely and living in the country, you make your own toys and invent your own games. I was in a world of make believe, under the big oak tree.

WHAT I LEARNED

1. I learned that I didn't need a lot of fancy toys, clothes, or electronics to have fun. I learned that I could use my imagination to invent games and toys, and have lots of exciting adventures.
2. I also learned that sometimes things can happen in life that try to stop me from having fun, but scary things don't last forever and problems aren't always as big as they seem.
3. I learned that having fancy clothes and expensive, popular toys does not always bring happiness.
4. I learned that having fear is a part of life, but it doesn't last forever.

WHAT DID YOU LEARN?

1. What is a fun game you like to play using your imagination?
2. Was there ever a time in your life when something bad happened that tried to stop your fun?
3. What are some things that make you happy?
4. What are some ways we can overcome our fears?

3

THE MOUSE IN THE ROYAL PALACE

Once upon a time there was a royal palace located on top of a very tall and beautiful mountain.

This palace had a King, a Queen, and many subjects under them. One day when everyone was busy working, there was an unexpected visitor in the palace. The maids were cleaning the King and Queen's chamber and low and behold, a mouse ran across the floor.

The maids screamed and jumped up on large chairs, terrified of the mouse. Then, the King and Queen came into the chamber, and the mouse headed right toward them. They both let out a loud scream, jumped up and down and their crowns fell off their heads and onto the floor. The maids opened the chamber door and slammed it behind them, leaving the King and Queen stranded in the chamber, screaming and running around in circles, fearful of the mouse.

Finally, the mouse vanished from sight. Days, months and years went by, and there was no sign of the mouse. The maids were happy the mouse was gone. The King and Queen were jubilant, and were so glad the mouse was gone, too.

All was well in the royal palace, until one stormy day, a flash of lightning passed through the King and Queen's chamber. It was followed by a loud crash of thunder that shook the foundation of the palace. The maids, the King, the Queen and guess who else? -- the mouse! -- came face to face. The mouse sat right smack in the middle of them.

Pandemonium broke out and everybody ran toward the chamber door. The mouse just stood there in the middle of the floor and watched, shaking his head. Then all of a sudden, the mouse said, "Wow! These people act like they've seen a ghost."

The maids, the King and the Queen heard the mouse talking and all said together, "Not just a mouse; but a *talking* mouse!" Now that the King and Queen were aware the mouse could talk, they came up with an idea.The King sent out a decree saying, "Here Ye Here Ye! We have a talking mouse in the palace and from this day forward, he will be our guest. His home will be in the walls of the palace, and no one will hurt or disturb him. Long live the mouse!"

WHAT I LEARNED

1. Even though this is just a make-believe story about a mouse in a palace, I learned a lot about how we as people treat each other.
2. I learned that most people are afraid of mice and feel that they are pests, but some people actually have mice as pets. This reminds me that not everyone is not afraid of mice.
3. I learned that you shouldn't form opinions about people or things before getting to know more about them.
4. I also learned sometimes, we don't give things or people a chance because of how they look. Just because they are different doesn't mean we are better than them.

WHAT DID YOU LEARN?

1. Have you ever had a bad thought about someone or something? What made you feel this way?
2. Have you ever thought you were better than someone else because they looked different? Do you think this is right? Why or why not?
3. Have you ever been afraid of something or someone because they looked different? Why or why not?
4. How do you treat people who look different than you?

4

THE LITTLE BOY WHO ALMOST FELL DOWN THE WELL

There was this little boy named Johnny who was about 4 years old.

He had just moved from the big city to live with his aunt and uncle in the country. One summer day, Johnny was playing in the backyard when he saw a wooden structure. Curious, he went over to see what it was.

To his amazement, there was a large hole in the center of the structure, so he climbed up on it to investigate. As he climbed up on the structure, he saw that the hole led somewhere; so he straddled the hole and began to get scared. It just so happened that his uncle was nearby and rushed over to pull Johnny up out of the structure.

This structure happened to be a well, and Johnny could have fallen down into it and drowned. This was the biggest scare of little Johnny's life. He learned a valuable lesson that day: Never climb into an open hole in the ground, especially if there's water in it.

Now when Johnny walks outside, he sees the well, but he knows not to climb on it. He's no longer afraid of drowning.

WHAT I LEARNED

1. I learned that just because I can do something, doesn't always mean it's safe.
2. I learned living in the country is so much different than in the city.
3. I learned that after my uncle pulled me off the well and gave me a stern talking to not to do it again, fear came over me, because I realized that I could have drowned.
4. I learned to not play on anything if I don't know what it is. Many children have accidently drowned playing in and around areas where there was water.

WHAT DID YOU LEARN?

1. Should your parents always know where you are? Why do you think this is?
2. Do your parents ever warn you of danger and that you can get hurt?
3. Do you listen to your parents when they tell you what not to do and where not to go?
4. Do your parents let you know they don't want you to get hurt? How do you feel about that?

5

DON'T TALK TO STRANGERS

When I was about 8 years old, a friend and I were walking down a country road. Two strangers in a car pulled over and attempted to make us get into the car. We refused immediately and began to walk away; in fact, our first instinct was to run as fast as we could through the woods, and we did exactly that. We ran so fast and didn't look back. My house was not too far from where the strangers tried to pick us up. When we arrived at my house, we explained to my mom what happened. She was very concerned, but happy that we escaped safely. Every time I visit home, I drive past that stretch of the road and can't forget the possible tragedy that could have occurred. It's the same road and the same woods we ran through to escape those two strangers. We could have been kidnapped or killed or abused. God was on our side and I'm so thankful as I reflect on this stretch of road and woods. My life has continued on after escaping two evil strangers, and I'm not afraid anymore.

WHAT I LEARNED

1. I learned to always be aware of my surroundings.
2. I learned never to stop and talk to a stranger.
3. I learned to walk away or run if a stranger insists on talking to me.
4. I learned to always let my parents know exactly where I am when I am playing outside.

WHAT DID YOU LEARN?

1. What would you do if you were approached by a stranger?
2. Is it ever OK to go somewhere with a stranger?
3. Would you scream or yell as loud as you could while you're running away?
4. What would you do if your surroundings looked unsafe or dangerous?

6

THE STORY OF THE BARKING DOG 🐶

There was this dog 🐶 who barked all the time, day and night.

He was always dependable, especially if intruders attempted to walk across the property. One day in broad daylight, an intruder walked up to the backyard and threw a big, fat, juicy steak in the yard. A brand-new riding lawnmower was parked inside a shed, and the intruder quickly and quietly strolled past the dog while he was occupied by the steak. The intruder then rushed back past the dog, pushing the lawnmower. The next day, the dog's owner got up bright and early to cut the grass, but to his surprise, he found an empty shed.

His brand new lawnmower was gone. Suddenly, fear came over him, because he knew someone had stolen his lawnmower. The owner looked angrily at the dog and said, "How did you let this happen?" The dog looked at his master, tail down and sadness in his eyes. His master continued to rant and rave, asking the dog again, "How did you let this happen?" Of course, the dog couldn't answer.

All he could do was keep his head down and his tail between his legs. The master was so enraged that he jumped up and down as he said to the dog, "You're fired! Expect to be picked up by the SPCA tomorrow and you're outta here. You're no longer dependable, and I'll get another dog that is!" The dog still didn't understand a word the owner was saying, but he knew it was bad.

All of a sudden, the dog started barking and the owner said, "Why are you barking now? It's too late to convince me to keep you."

While the owner was out back with the dog, the front of his home was being broken into, and the intruders wiped him out in a matter of minutes. The dog continued to bark, and the owner continued to tell the dog that it was too late, that he was not changing his mind. Finally, the owner walked back into the house, where he immediately discovered that his house had been ransacked and many items were gone. It hit him like a ton of bricks. Now, he finally realized why the dog had been barking as the man was fussing and firing him, so he decided to give the dog another chance. They became very close, and the owner was not afraid anymore because his best friend, the dog, was there to warn and protect him.

WHAT I LEARNED

1. I learned to appreciate others (friends and family) who are there for me.
2. I learned not to be so quick to put others down when they make mistakes.
3. I learned to be thankful for friends who stick up for me.
4. I learned to love my friends despite their flaws or mistakes.

WHAT DID YOU LEARN?

1. Do you have friends or family who will stick by you? How do you know?
2. Why do friends put other friends down?
3. Do you ever talk mean to your friends? Can you explain why you think this is right?
4. Do you appreciate your friends? What do you appreciate about them?

7

THE CAT WHO ATE THE RAT

Miss Lucy! Miss Lucy! How are you doing? ...

I got this sick cat, who ate a rat. Every time I say "scat," he says "rat." I said to myself, "What's the matter with that cat?" Every time I say "scat," he says "rat," so I picked up the sick cat and he felt very fat. I said, "Cat, why are you so fat?" The cat said, "'Cause I ate a rat." So I squeezed the cat's stomach and out jumped a rat. Wouldn't you know, the rat was still alive? I was so afraid. I said to the cat, "Why is this rat still alive?" And the cat said, "I swallowed him whole while you were outside hanging up clothes." Then Miss Lucy told the cat to scat. So the cat looked around for the rat, but the rat was long gone.

The cat became sad, because there were no more rats to eat. So he said to himself, "I know what! I'll go next door to my neighbors' house and see if there are any rats there." The cat scratched on the neighbor's door and when the neighbor saw that it was a cat, the neighbor said, "Scat, cat!" The cat said to the neighbor, "I don't mean any harm, I just wanna know if you have any rats?" So the neighbor said, "Well, I got one that just came around." And the cat said, "I can get rid of him if you want." The neighbor said to the cat, "That would be a great help." So the neighbor let the cat in, and the cat began to roam the house in search of the rat. Low and behold, out stepped the same rat that he had swallowed whole.The cat said to

himself, "This time I'll get him."
By this time, the rat was a few steps ahead of the cat. The rat left the house and went on to the next neighbor.

When the cat found out the rat was gone, he said to himself, "I'm getting tired of chasing after this rat! It ain't worth it. I'm going back home to let my master know the rat is gone." When the cat got home, he told his master the rat was gone and he wouldn't have to worry or be afraid any more. The master breathed a sigh of relief, happy the rat was no longer around.

WHAT I LEARNED

1. I learned that some things in life are not worth chasing after.
2. I learned to focus on what my purpose in life is.
3. I learned not to be so quick to condemn others.
4. I learned how to think before making a move.

WHAT DID YOU LEARN?

1. What are some things in life that are important to you?
2. What do you do when you want things that your parents say you cannot have?
3. Have you ever eaten anything you didn't like and it made you sick?
4. Have you ever disliked someone that you really didn't know? Why did you dislike them?

8

THE LITTLE RED WAGON

When I was a kid, I always dreamed of having a little red wagon. Being raised in the country, we used wood-burning stoves for cooking and heating. One of my chores was to cut up the wood for burning in the stoves. The woodpile was quite a distance from the house, and I had to carry it one armful at a time, even during bad weather. I remember seeing a little red wagon in a department store one day. I wished so very hard to own one. "I could use it for hauling my wood from the woodpile to the porch," I thought to myself. If I had this little red wagon, I could pretend that I was hauling logs or lumber. I could also use the wagon to haul food from the barn to the hog pen. I had high expectations that one day I would own a little red wagon, but sadly, it never happened. We were so poor that my parents could not afford to buy one, so I continued to carry armfuls of wood from the woodpile to the porch. One day I thought to myself, "I know what I'll do! I'll make my own wagon to haul my wood. So I took a couple boards and nailed them together. I found two axles and four wheels from a worn-out baby carriage and attached them to the boards. I used large staples to hold the axles onto the wood. I nailed a long piece of rope to the board in order to pull the wagon. Finally, I had my own homemade wagon. Of course, it wasn't the little red wagon that I longed for, but it was better than carrying wood in my arms. Whenever I see a red wagon, even as an adult, it reminds me of the little red wagon that I never had.

WHAT I LEARNED

1. I learned that every dream does not always come true.
2. I learned to never give up on my dreams.
3. I learned that life can sometimes bring disappointments.
4. I learned that sometimes dreams do come true.

WHAT DID YOU LEARN?

1. Have you ever had dreams that didn't come true? How does that make you feel?
2. What are some ways we can reach for our dreams?
3. How do you handle disappointment?
4. Do you ever share your dreams and goals with your parents?

CLOSING REFLECTIONS

I wrote this book to share some of my childhood experiences and life lessons with children. Children need guidance, direction and encouragement. This book will help give them a better understanding of how to overcome some of the problems they will experience growing up. For example, fear is a normal part of life, but children can be taught how to overcome it, just like the characters in the stories. My goal is for children to enjoy each story and be inspired by the lessons. I hope to share this book with as many children as possible all over the world to help them remember my stories and learn how to apply valuable lessons to their lives.

ABOUT THE AUTHOR

John Powell was born in Norfolk, Virginia; one of six siblings. At age 4, he moved to Sunbury, North Carolina, to live with his aunt and uncle. Sunbury was a very small town mainly consisting of farming and logging as its main source of income. John's childhood life was centered around a rural country setting where the family raised chickens, ducks, geese and hogs.

At age 18, John attended Norfolk State University and graduated with a bachelor's degree in industrial arts education. It wasn't until years later in John's life that he became interested in writing poetry as well as children's stories.

"My passion is for children of the younger generation to learn from my many experiences as a child growing up; they have a rich history and legacy. I want children to stretch their imaginations without the crutch of social media and electronics to engage in their originality and creativity. I'm also passionate about our children becoming socially aware and learning to empathize with others who may be different from them. My goal is to help children think outside of the box and reach their highest potential in life."

John

About the Publishing Support Services:

Motivational M.D. Publishing is a family-owned publishing company that assists aspiring authors to publish books that heal, uplift, and inspire. It was founded by Dr. Jasmine Zapata, who is an award-winning author, public health physician, empowerment speaker, mother, and wife. You can connect with the Motivational M.D. Publishing team here: www.motivationalmdpublishing.com

Made in the USA
Middletown, DE
19 February 2022

61350925R00033